Tiger Walk

Story by **Dianne Hofmeyr**
Pictures by **Jesse Hodgson**

Otter-Barry BOOKS

At the art gallery, Tom watches the tiger.
And the tiger watches Tom. From between
the jungly leaves, his eyes follow Tom around the room.

Back home, Tom grabs some crayons
and a piece of paper.

He draws the tiger **BIG**...
with pointy teeth and a swishing tail
and green-jewel eyes.

That night, shadows creep around Tom's room.
Dark and scary.
From the wall, the tiger's green-jewel eyes
stare back at him.
The whiskers twitch.
The tail swishes.
Tom holds his breath.

The tiger steps forward.
It pads closer. . .
and closer. . .
UNTIL. . .

Tom feels the hot tigery breath against his cheek.

"Lets go for a walk," the tiger purrs.

"But it's night-time. And it's very dark!" whispers Tom.

"Tigers aren't scared of the dark. Besides, there's a moon.

Climb up. Hold tight."

So Tom climbs on the tiger's back.

He smells the hot tigery smell.

Then out they pad, into the gleaming jungle of the night,

until they come to a forest that drips with moonflowers.

And everywhere they see foxes
and bears and even a lion.

"I'm a little bit scared of foxes and bears and lions," Tom whispers. "They have pointy teeth. And sharp claws."

"We'll play!" smiles the tiger, showing his pointy teeth and his swishing tail.

So they do.

They play hide-and-seek between the trees...

UNTIL. . .

they come to a river.

"How will we get to the other side?" whispers Tom.

"We'll swim," growls the tiger.

"I'm a little bit scared of swimming," says Tom.
"The river looks deep. And there might be eels."

"Tigers love swimming. Tigers aren't scared of eels.
I'll swat them away with my paws.

Hold tight!"

So Tom holds tight.

Down, down they dive.

And their breath comes out in bubbles.

And the moonlight shines silver on the pebbles.

And everywhere there are fish and even eels…

UNTIL. . .

on the other side of the river
they come to a fair.

"A fair? I'm a little bit scared of fairs,"
whispers Tom. "There are ghost trains
and merry-go-rounds and swings
that go too high."

"Tigers aren't scared of ghost trains
or swings that go too high. Hold tight!"

So Tom does.
And around and around they fly.

Faster. . .

and faster. . .

UNTIL. . .

they are high above the world
and close to the stars.

"How will we ever get back?" whispers Tom.

"I know the way," growls the tiger. "Hold tight!"

And off they fly through the frozen sky.

"I'm a little bit scared of flying. It's very cold.
And there could be a blizzard."

"Tigers aren't scared of blizzards," snarls the tiger.
"Besides, there's a cave we can hide in."

Down they swoop and come to a cave
with arches of ice and frozen waterfalls
and icicles that crackle as they move.

In the middle are two huge tigers carved of ice...

EXCEPT...

they are REAL!

"TIGERS! I'm VERY scared of tigers!"

"No, you're NOT!" snaps the tiger. "I'M a tiger!
Besides, these are snow tigers and snow tigers
love to dance. We'll light a fire and we'll dance."

The tigers step forward. They shake the ice
from their whiskers and dance a tigery dance
in the firelight, with frosty breath and swishing tails
and flashing eyes.

Tom dances too.

Faster...

and faster...

UNTIL...

he's too tired to dance any more.

"It's time to go home," says the tiger.

So away they fly, through the frozen sky.
And before Tom knows it, they are back home.

Tom lies between the tigery paws
and the tigery claws
and yawns a big yawn.

"I don't think I'm scared any more."

"Not scared?" the tiger purrs.

Tom shakes his head. "No! I'm not scared of anything.
Perhaps... **I'm a tiger!**"

He snuggles against the tiger and closes his eyes...
and falls fast asleep.

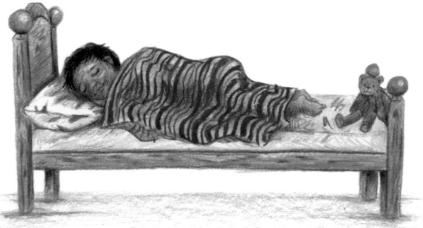

About Henri Rousseau

The painting Tom saw in the gallery was *Surprised!* (sometimes called *Tiger in a Tropical Storm)*, by Henri Rousseau,
which hangs in the National Gallery in London. It was painted in 1891, and was one of Henri Rousseau's
first 'jungle' paintings. In the painting lightning flashes, rain comes pelting down,
trees and grasses sway, while the tiger crouches and snarls.

Henri Rousseau was born in France in 1844. He became known for painting 'dream' visions of
jungle scenes with wild animals peering through leaves and exotic flowers, but he never once had
a painting lesson, nor did he ever leave France and see a real jungle. He got all his ideas from
the Jardin des Plantes (the Botanical Garden in Paris) and from books and magazines
and by visiting the Zoo. He said, 'I have no teacher but nature.'

Rousseau only became truly famous after his death in 1910, when other artists like Picasso began to appreciate
his imaginary, dream-like work. Now his paintings are in gallery collections around the world.
Two famous pictures, *The Dream* and *The Sleeping Gypsy*, hang in the Museum of Modern Art in New York.

For Jack, the bravest boy I know – DH

For two bold tigers, Kate and Anna – JH

Text copyright © Dianne Hofmeyr 2018
Illustrations copyright © Jesse Hodgson 2018

The right of Dianne Hofmeyr and Jesse Hodgson to be identified, respectively, as the author
and illustrator of this work has been asserted by them in accordance with the Copyright,
Designs and Patents Act, 1988 (United Kingdom).
Surprised! Henri Rousseau © The National Gallery, London

First published in Great Britain in 2018 and in the USA in 2019 by
Otter-Barry Books
Little Orchard, Burley Gate, Hereford, HR1 3QS

www.otterbarrybooks.com

A catalogue record for this book is available from the British Library.

ISBN 978-1-91095-941-1

Illustrated with coloured pencils

Printed in China

1 3 5 7 9 8 6 4 2